A CHANCE TO SHINE

by STEVE SESKIN &
ALLEN SHAMBLIN

Illustrations by

R. GREGORY CHRISTIE

Tricycle Press * Berkeley / Toronto

Joe smelled kind of funny. He was a little bit weird.
He wore trash can shoes, had a scraggly beard.
He'd talk to the pigeons in front of Dad's store.
I often wondered what he was sitting there for.

One day Dad said, "Joe, I'll make you a deal.
Sweep the sidewalk each morning and you can count on your meals."
Joe stood up straight and shook my dad's hand.

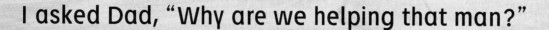

I asked Dad, "Why are we helping that man?"

And Dad said, "Every heart needs a chance to shine,
to be wanted by someone somewhere down the line.
We're all meant to write on the pages of time."

Every heart just needs a chance to shine.

Joe showed up next morning showered and shaved.
I almost didn't recognize him when he smiled and waved.
He tackled that sidewalk with a broom and a plan.
I followed him around with Momma's dustpan.

Dad said he'd never seen that sidewalk so clean.
Joe ate three plates of chicken and two bowls of beans.

A few weeks more of sweeping and next thing you know,
Dad let me be stock boy and my new boss was Joe.

By the end of that summer he was back on his feet.
He'd rented an apartment just down the street.

One day Dad said as we walked by Joe's place,
"The beginning of greatness from a once hopeless case."

When I went back to school, something had changed.
I was hanging out with kids I used to call strange.

My old friends asked me why. I said I really don't know.
I just look at people differently since I met this guy Joe.
Then I'd tell them the story, how we got to know this man,
how he and my dad helped me understand...

Every heart needs a chance to shine,
to be wanted by someone somewhere down the line.
We're all meant to write on the pages of time.

Every heart just needs
a chance to shine.

A CHANCE TO SHINE

To all those who, when faced with difficult circumstances, find a way to rise above them, and to those kind souls who help them to do so. I'd like to thank my family as well.
—SS

To my parents, Jim and Alice Shamblin, who worked hard to give their children "a chance to shine."
—AS

For Janet and Jenny.   —RGC

Text copyright © 2006 by Steve Seskin and Allen Shamblin
Illustrations copyright © 2006 by R. Gregory Christie

Original version of "A Chance to Shine" written by Steve Seskin and Allen Shamblin © 1991 by Sony/ATV Music • David Aaron Music • BMG Music • Universal Music

The publisher wishes to thank Robert Puff of RPM Seattle Music Preparation for drafting the musical score.

Tricycle Press
a little division of Ten Speed Press
P.O. Box 7123
Berkeley, California 94707
www.tricyclepress.com

Design by Betsy Stromberg
Typeset in Josef and Grotesque
The illustrations in this book were rendered in acrylic.

The enclosed compact disc includes two tracks of "A Chance to Shine" performed by Steve Seskin and Allen Shamblin. If you'd like to reach Steve Seskin or hear more of his recordings, go to www.steveseskin.com. You can correspond with Allen Shamblin at www.allenshamblin.com.

Library of Congress Cataloging-in-Publication Data

Seskin, Steve.
  A chance to shine / by Steve Seskin and Allen Shamblin ; illustrations by R. Gregory Christie.
    p. cm.
  Summary: A child's father changes the life of a homeless man by giving him a job.
  ISBN-13: 978-1-58246-167-0
  ISBN-10: 1-58246-167-8
  [1. Homeless persons—Fiction. 2. Conduct of life—Fiction. 3. Fathers—Fiction. 4. Stories in rhyme.] I. Shamblin, Allen. II. Christie, Gregory, 1971- ill. III. Title.
  PZ8.3+
  [E]—dc22

First Tricycle Press printing, 2006
Printed in China

1 2 3 4 5 6 — 10 09 08 07 06

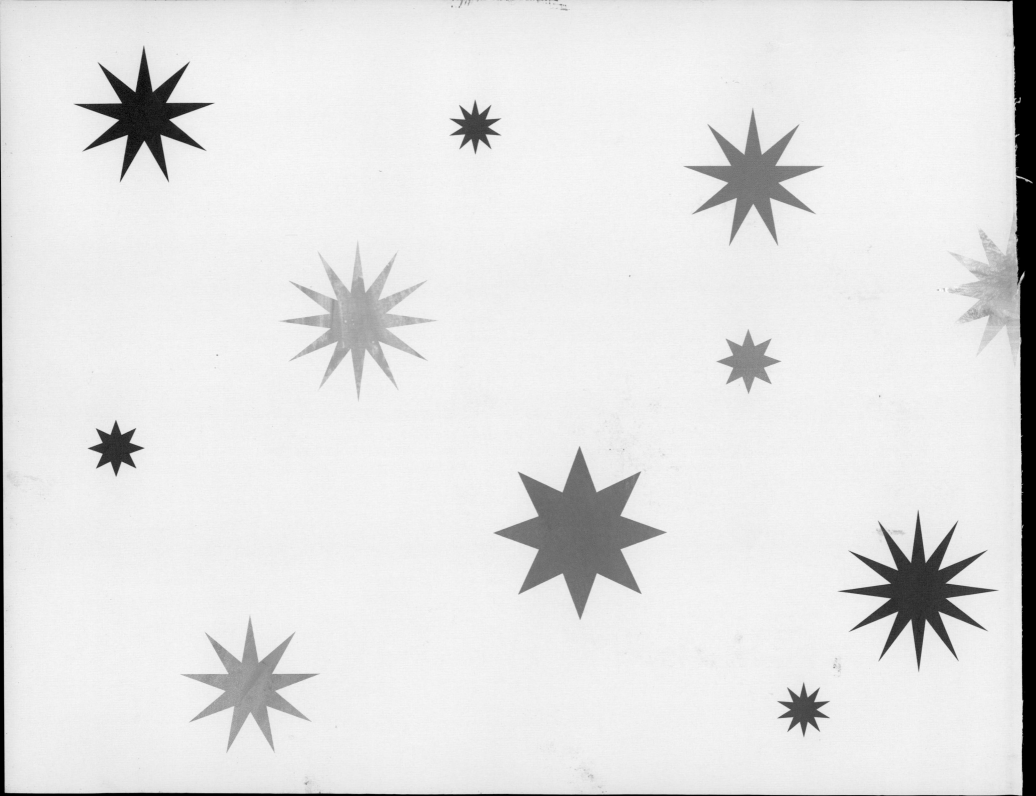